© STRÖVA
King Elk
Project manager: Lena Allblom, IKEA of Sweden AB
Project coordinator: Anders Truedsson, TITEL Books AB
Text: Ulf Stark
Illustrations: Ann-Cathrine Sigrid Ståhlberg
Typesetting: Gyllene Snittet AB, Sweden
Translation: Comactiva Language Partner AB, Sweden
Produced by IKEA of Sweden AB
Paper: Arcoset FSC
Printing: Litopat S.p.A., Italy 2013
TITEL Books AB for IKEA of Sweden AB. All rights reserved.

THE LIBRARY GHOST

Carole Boston Weatherford

Illustrations by Lee White

Fort Atkinson, Wisconsin
www.upstartbooks.com

*In memory of my grandfather, the Reverend Lun P. Whitten,
who believed in ghosts.*

To Gloria Johnston, the school librarian who believed in me.
—C. B. W.

To Machiko, Ken, and Gene.
—L. W.

The riddle, "What gallops for miles but leaves not a track" is a reference to "The Railway Train." from
Emily Dickinson: Selected Poems by Emily Dickinson. Dover Publications, 1990.

Published by UpstartBooks
W5527 State Road 106
P.O. Box 800
Fort Atkinson, Wisconsin 53538-0800
1-800-448-4887

Text © 2008 by Carole Boston Weatherford
Illustrations © 2008 by Lee White

The paper used in this publication meets the minimum requirements of American
National Standard for Information Science — Permanence of Paper for Printed Library
Material. ANSI/NISO Z39.48.

The library by day was busy and bright,
But after the doors were closed for the night

And the guard dozed off after checking the locks,
The halls were abuzz with bumps, thuds, and knocks.

Each morning the librarian found a big mess—
Books helter-skelter, piled high on desks.

Ms. Mims was stumped as she went shelf by shelf
And concluded, "I'd best do a night shift myself."
When the last reader left, she set several traps
And stayed on the lookout between her catnaps.

But the library ghost had but one task in mind:
To search every book until she could find
The one thing she lacked to at last rest in peace;
So she flipped through the atlas—north, south, west, and east.

She looked inside fairy tales, fables, and novels,
Grilled ogres and giants until they groveled.

She cornered Jack Horner, pinned down Peter Pan,
And quizzed the Mad Hatter of Wonderland.

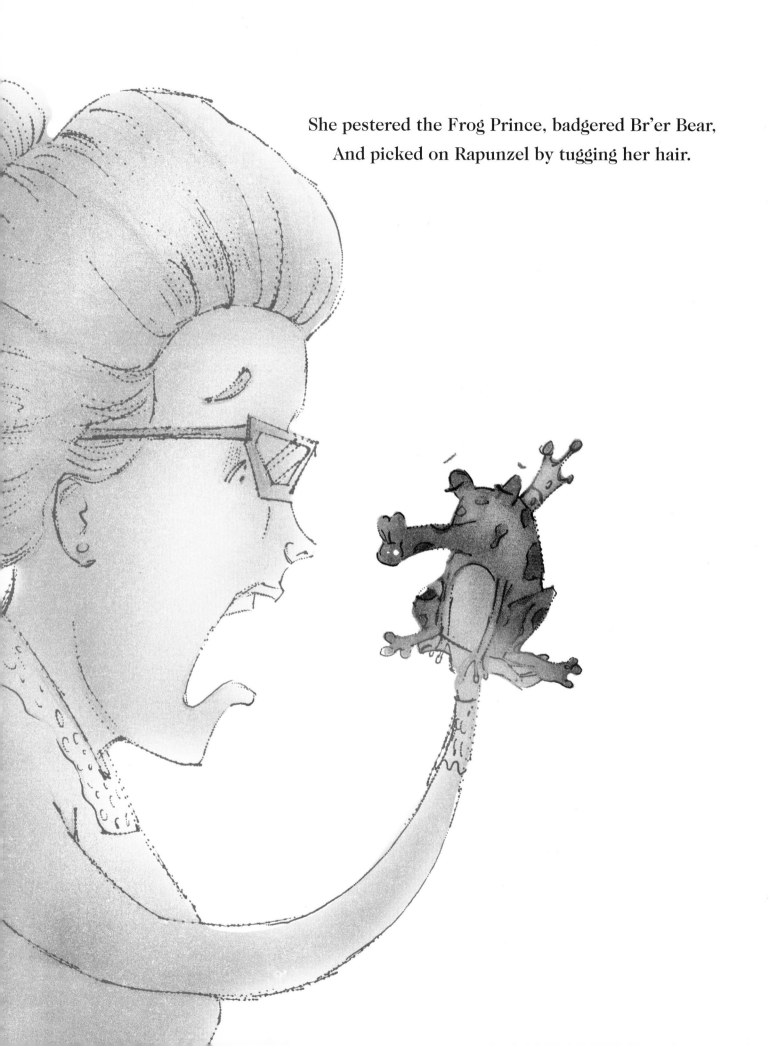

She pestered the Frog Prince, badgered Br'er Bear,
And picked on Rapunzel by tugging her hair.

She begged the Good Witch
and the Wizard of Oz
And shook the brass lamp
where the genie was.

She spooked Rumplestiltskin and Billy Goats Gruff,
Bugged the Bad Wolf who stormed off in a huff,
Poked Rip Van Winkle, woke him from a dream,
And frightened Miss Muffet who let out a scream.

Ms. Mims heard the ruckus and leapt from her chair,
Rushed down the hallway and up a dark stair.

Face to face with the ghost, she shook off her fear,
Said, "Shhhhh!" and then asked, "What are you doing here?"

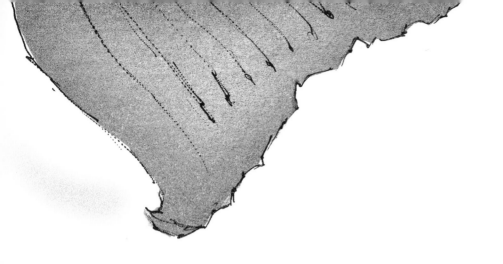

The guilt-ridden ghost said, "I just cannot rest."
Ms. Mims stared her down and said, "Let me guess.
You wrote in a book or tore out page nine.
You brought books back late and still owe a fine."

The ghost hung her head, "You must think I'm a jerk.
I let someone down needing help with homework.
I was stumped by a riddle, a hard-to-find fact:
What gallops for miles but leaves not a track?"

Then, it came to Ms. Mims, the ghost was Miss Hall,
The woman whose portrait hangs on the wall,
The librarian who manned the old reference desk
And tackled each question like some kind of test.

"Let's search the Web, dear," said Ms. Mims with a sigh,
And a freight train appeared in the blink of an eye.

No longer in limbo, the ghost grabbed a book
And perched herself right in the storytime nook.

Amid pillows and plush toys, she sits to this day,
Reading book after book and there plans to stay.
When Ms. Mims shares ghost lore, kids know it is true
For the library ghost ends each tale with a "BOO!"